Maggie and Pie
and the Big Breakfast

By Carolyn Cory Scoppettone
Art by Paula J. Becker

HIGHLIGHTS PRESS
Honesdale, Pennsylvania

Stories + Puzzles = Reading Success!

Dear Parents,

Highlights Puzzle Readers are an innovative approach to learning to read that combines puzzles and stories to build motivated, confident readers.

Developed in collaboration with reading experts, the stories and puzzles are seamlessly integrated so that readers are encouraged to read the story, solve the puzzles, and then read the story again. This helps increase vocabulary and reading fluency and creates a satisfying reading experience for any kind of learner. In addition, solving puzzles fosters important reading and learning skills such as:

- shape and letter recognition
- letter-sound relationships
- visual discrimination
- logic
- flexible thinking
- sequencing

With high-interest stories, humorous characters, and trademark puzzles, Highlights Puzzle Readers offer a winning combination for inspiring young learners to love reading.

This is Maggie.

This is Pie.

Maggie and Pie love to **cook**.
But sometimes Maggie
gets a little **mixed up**.

You can help by
using the clues
to find the supplies
they need.

Happy reading!

The sun peeks over the hill.

"I am hungry," says Maggie.
"Can we make a big breakfast?"

"Yes," says Pie. "Here is a recipe.
We can make applesauce pancakes.
First, we need the batter."

"I can get it," says Maggie.

"Why are you dressed like that?"
asks Pie.

"You said we need a batter,"
says Maggie.

"Oh no," sighs Pie.

"We need *pancake* batter."

"The pancake mix is in a red box.
It is on the middle shelf.
It is the biggest box on that shelf.
Can you find it?" asks Pie.

"Here is the pancake mix!"
says Maggie.

"Thanks," says Pie.
"Now we need ground cinnamon."

"I can get it," says Maggie.

"What are you doing?" asks Pie.

"I am looking on the ground,"
says Maggie.

"Oh no," sighs Pie.
"Ground cinnamon is not
on the ground."

"The cinnamon is in a brown tin.

It is on the bottom shelf.

It is on top of a yellow box.

Can you find it?" asks Pie.

"Here is the cinnamon!" says Maggie.

"Thanks," says Pie.
"Now we need applesauce."

"I can get it," says Maggie.

"Here are apples," says Maggie.

"And here is sauce!"

"Oh no," sighs Pie.

"We do not need tomato sauce."

"The applesauce is in a pink jar.

It is next to a blue box.

It is not next to a green jar.

Can you find it?" asks Pie.

"Here is the applesauce!" says Maggie.

"Thanks," says Pie.
"Now I will mix the batter."

"I will make the frosting," says Maggie.

"Why do we need frosting?" asks Pie.

"For the cakes!" says Maggie.

"We can frost them in the pan."

"Oh no," sighs Pie.

"We do not eat pancakes with frosting.

We eat them with maple syrup."

"I can find the maple syrup,"
says Maggie.

"Where are you going?" asks Pie.

"I am going to find a maple tree,"
says Maggie.

"Oh no," sighs Pie.

"The maple syrup is not in a tree.

It is in the fridge."

"The syrup is in a brown bottle.

It is on the shelf with the eggs.

It is next to an orange bottle.

Can you find it?" asks Pie.

"Here is the syrup!" says Maggie.

"Thanks," says Pie.

"Now we need a plate."

"I can get it," says Maggie.

"Here is a plate," says Maggie.

"Oh no," sighs Pie.
"We need a breakfast plate,
not a home plate."

Maggie and Pie eat some pancakes.

But they cannot eat them all.

"I think we made too many,"
says Maggie.

"What can we do with them?"

"We can throw a pancake party for our friends," says Pie.

"I know just what we need," says Maggie.

"Why do we need that?" asks Pie.

"If we are *throwing* a party,"
says Maggie, "I need my lucky glove."

"Oh no," sighs Pie.

"Why not?" asks Maggie.

"We have a bat, a plate, and a glove.

After we eat the pancakes,

we can play baseball!"

Applesauce Pancakes

MAKES 12 PANCAKES

Wash your hands or wings!

You Need

- 1½ cups all-purpose flour
- 1 tablespoon baking powder
- 1 tablespoon sugar
- ½ teaspoon salt
- ½ teaspoon cinnamon
- 1 cup unsweetened applesauce
- ¾ cup milk
- 1 teaspoon vanilla extract
- Cooking spray, oil, or butter
- Maple syrup (optional!)

1. Stir.

Stir together the **flour, baking powder, sugar, salt,** and **cinnamon** in a large bowl.

2. Pour.

Pour the **applesauce, milk,** and **vanilla** into the bowl.

3. Mix.

Mix everything together until just combined. Lumps are okay!

4. Rest.

Let the batter rest for 5 minutes.

ADULT: Lightly grease a large heavy pan or griddle with cooking spray, oil, or butter.

5. Scoop.

Scoop ¼ cup batter onto the pan for each pancake. A 10-inch pan will fit 3 pancakes.

ADULT: Gently flatten the top with a rubber spatula. Cook over medium heat until bubbly on the surface and slightly dry on the edges, 2 to 3 minutes. Flip and cook for another 2 to 3 minutes until golden.

Do you like maple syrup on your pancakes like Pie does?

For information about permission to reprint
selections from this book, please contact
permissions@highlights.com.

Published by Highlights Press
815 Church Street
Honesdale, Pennsylvania 18431
ISBN (paperback): 978-64472-477-4
ISBN (hardcover): 978-64472-478-1
ISBN (ebook): 978-64472-479-8

Library of Congress Control Number: 2021938020
Printed in Melrose Park, IL, USA
Mfg. 08/2021
First edition
Visit our website at Highlights.com.
10 9 8 7 6 5 4 3 2 1

Recipe by Pat Tanumihardja

This book has been officially leveled by using the
F&P Text Level Gradient™ Leveling System.

LEXILE®, LEXILE FRAMEWORK®,
LEXILE ANALYZER®, the LEXILE®
logo and POWERV® are trademarks c
MetaMetrics, Inc., and are registered
in the United States and abroad. The
trademarks and names of other companies and
products mentioned herein are the property of thei
respective owners. Copyright © 2021 MetaMetrics,
Inc. All rights reserved.

For assistance in the preparation of this book,
the editors would like to thank Julie Tyson, MSEd
Reading, MSEd Administration K–12, Title 1 Reading
Specialist; and Gina Shaw.